A Set of Wings

PRAISE FOR *STORYSHARES*

"One of the brightest innovators and game-changers in the education industry."
– Forbes

"Your success in applying research-validated practices to promote literacy serves as a valuable model for other organizations seeking to create evidence-based literacy programs."

- Library of Congress

"We need powerful social and educational innovation, and Storyshares is breaking new ground. The organization addresses critical problems facing our students and teachers. I am excited about the strategies it brings to the collective work of making sure every student has an equal chance in life."
– Teach For America

"Around the world, this is one of the up-and-coming trailblazers changing the landscape of literacy and education."
- International Literacy Association

"It's the perfect idea. There's really nothing like this. I mean wow, this will be a wonderful experience for young people."   - Andrea Davis Pinkney, Executive Director, Scholastic

"Reading for meaning opens opportunities for a lifetime of learning. Providing emerging readers with engaging texts that are designed to offer both challenges and support for each individual will improve their lives for years to come. Storyshares is a wonderful start."
- David Rose, Co-founder of CAST & UDL

A Set of Wings

Linda Peng

STORYSHARES

Story Share, Inc.
New York. Boston. Philadelphia

Storyshares
Story Share, Inc.
24 N. Bryn Mawr Avenue #340
Bryn Mawr, PA 19010-3304
www.storyshares.org

Inspiring reading with a new kind of book.

Interest Level: Middle School
Grade Level Equivalent: 3.7

9781642611885

Book design by Storyshares

Printed in the United States of America

Storyshares Presents

1

Sheltered—that's what I am. When I look in the mirror, which is rarely an activity I enjoy, I see a pale boy who represents so little. There is nothing with which to define myself. My parents believe I am an inspiration. Something about continuing to fight this cursed disease that plagues me. But inspirations don't sit around the house all day, scared to go out and unwilling to come back in. My freedom is a short chain.

When you stay in the house all day, you notice things about it. The places you never go are forgotten. They fade into the recesses of memory. The places you do go become haunted; they embrace you with imprisoning comfort, keeping you safe and suffocated.

This morning, I am almost too lethargic to crack open my eyes. Through my blinds, weak sunlight illuminates the drifting dust particles in the room. The rest of the small, dingy room remains in shadow. I stare blankly at the dresser at the foot of my bed, which seems to stare straight back at me, unmoving. To my right, homework is strewn atop my desk beside the gloomy little lamp. A black swivel chair is parked at the workspace with my old jacket hanging off it. I breathe in, breathe out, and then close my eyes. For a moment, I'd hoped this reality had only been a nightmare, but my reality has not changed.

Quiet rapping at my door rouses me. This time, I don't even bother to open my eyes. The rapping repeats a few more times. Then I hear the squeak of my doorknob and the groan of the rusty door hinges as it opens.

"Andrew? Are you awake?"

It's my mom. She takes a few steps into the room and hesitates. "Andrew? It's past noon."

"I don't want to get up," I mumble.

"Honey, I know you're tired, but staying in bed all day won't make you feel better."

I roll over and open my eyes to squint at her. "What day is it?"

She smiles slightly. "Saturday. We've got a surprise planned for you this weekend, remember?"

I roll the other way, putting my back to her. "I'll just be fifteen minutes."

She hesitates again. My parents, beyond not knowing what to do with me, also no longer know how to address me. They think that if they are too harsh with their words, I'll fall over and shatter.

"Then I'll see you downstairs." Another pause. "Be careful, Andrew."

2

When I finally go downstairs, I'm greeted by my family. They're seated for breakfast, and the smell of bacon and pancakes wafts toward me. My mom quickly puts down her cup of coffee, and her face lights up when she sees me. She beckons to the chair next to her.

On her other side is an empty chair with Dad's coffee cup in front of it. He is at the stove, sliding a fluffy pancake onto the rapidly growing stack. He lowers his spatula and winks at me, then brings the tower of pancakes to the table. Christian, my older brother by two years, is seated closest to me. By the look of his syrup-drowned plate, he has already eaten a small mountain of pancakes. I frown at everyone's bright expressions and take a seat, ignoring the elbow Christian nudges me with.

"Hey, Andy, what's up?" he asks.

I pick up my fork and glare at him. "Don't call me that."

Christian grins. "Fine, Andrew. Are you excited for today?"

I spear a bite of pancake and contemplate it. I used to love pancakes. Now, I set it down and glare at my brother. "What's today?"

"You'll see," he says excitedly.

His good mood makes me more irritated, and I quickly push his comment out of my thoughts. I slide past breakfast with as little eating as possible and gulp down some water before trudging back toward my room.

"Andrew, wait!" Mom calls.

I turn back and glance at her, annoyed. "Yes?"

"We have a surprise for you."

"So I've heard," I mutter. "What is it?"

"We've decided you need to get out of town for a bit," Dad butts in, smiling at me. "Go pack a bag for two nights. We'll be loading the car."

"Wh—what . . ." I stutter. "But I don't . . . I don't want to."

"You need some fresh air!" Mom pipes up.

"Are we . . . leaving right now?" I continue. I don't know whether to be grateful or terrified. "Where are we going?"

Mom beams at me. "We want to be on the road in an hour. You'll enjoy it where we're going, I promise. It's a surprise. You'll be able to get back outside! You never leave the house anymore."

I make a face at her. "Oh? I thought I just wasn't allowed."

Mom winces. "Honey, of course not." She hesitates for a moment, knowing that I must be as anxious about my own health as she is. "Don't worry about the trip being too taxing. I've checked with Dr. Martin and made arrangements with the local hospital in case you don't feel well once we head out. You don't need to worry about a thing."

I nod slowly. "I don't have a choice about this, do I?"

Christian comes up behind me and nudges me toward my room. "Nope, you don't! Get ready, let's go! It's time for you to see a little bit of the world."

3

I can't decide whether to be annoyed or excited as we pull out of the driveway. So I decide on the grey area in between: disinterested. My nonchalance soon turns into boredom, which quickly allows the familiar dark cloud to settle over me again. To counter the feeling, I stuff in my earbuds to drown out the world. Ignoring people is one thing I am good at, and fifteen years of experience helps.

I wonder if this trip is supposed to help me be more social. Half of me hopes not, and the other half admits I kind of need some help—and some friends. I notice my mom shooting me glances in the rearview mirror. They're talking about the destination. I wedge one earbud out of my ear and gaze out the window.

"It'll be nice and quiet for him," Mom is saying. "Something new and peaceful. Maybe he'll even want to come back."

"New?" Dad sighs. "I'm worried, Jeannette. How do you know the hotel won't be just like the house for him? He won't have anyone new to talk to."

No people, I think to myself. I feel relief accompanied by just a pinch of regret.

"We'll get him out of his room," Mom says. "What about sightseeing? There are so many beautiful landmarks in the wilderness."

"Sightseeing? We don't want to tire him out."

"Just a little! We'll stay close to the car and far from the mountain. Nothing strenuous."

My heart falls. Of course they would never let me go climbing. It's too risky. I shove my earbud back in with frustration and let the music drown out my thoughts.

"We're here!" Christian chirps, tugging the cord away from my face. I jerk away from him and glare as he unplugs my music. "Take a look, Andrew!"

The gravel parking lot we're in faces what must be a hotel. It's a large, cozy looking rendition of a cottage one would expect to find in a fairy tale. Small, sleepy windows peer at me from the upper floor. The entire establishment is a warm brown, with ivy creeping up every wall. Behind it, there's a sweep of forest that rolls out from a towering mountain.

I groan and lean back into my seat. Nothing here is allowed for me. I can't even go hiking. I'm sure I'd trip, fall, and die. It's all I've been hearing, ever since I could understand that I was in an extremely weak condition. They all try to protect me, as if by staying safe I'll be rewarded with another year of life.

"Let's go!" Christian roars in my ear.

I push him away and slide out of the car. With a sigh, I head into the resort's restaurant for a measly lunch laden with pills—the usual.

I feel a tap on my shoulder before I'm even done eating, and I don't have the energy to be annoyed. I never have an appetite anyway, not since I've been diagnosed.

All food has lost its flavor. I turn around to see my brother with a devilish smile on his face.

"C'mon, let's go unpack," he suggests.

I shrug and get up, too miserable to care. *To pack or not to pack?* I had asked myself a dozen times before leaving, only to grab a heap of clothes and dump them into the suitcase a minute later. I'd been so distracted wondering if Hamlet had questioned his clothing choices before being sent off to England that I'm sure I didn't even remember to bring underwear.

"Don't let him lift anything too heavy," Mom says to Christian. Her reminder makes me feel like throwing something. If I can't lift anything heavier than a toothbrush, what are they keeping me alive for? I decide that "To be, or not to be" is, in fact, the question. I get up and follow my brother.

4

I keep my head down as I walk behind Christian to the elevator, not wanting to face the stares people give me when they notice how pale I am. Christian moves with confidence: head up, shoulders back. My brother has always been healthy. More than healthy, he's spectacular. Sports, school, extracurricular activities. If there is something to succeed in, he's done it.

I would be jealous, but what for? I can only stick to what I know. Christian has always been spontaneous, too. Never boring. And he understands how I feel about Mom and Dad, their constant worrying. Christian tries to convince them that I'm strong enough to do the same things everyone else does, but it hasn't worked so far. My parents want to monitor my every move. There is always a sentence that starts off with "just in case" that no one wants to finish.

We climb inside the elevator, my breath quickening at the small space. Apparently, I'm too fragile to take the stairs, so the elevator is my only choice. Christian stabs a few buttons, and I glance up at the metal panel. We weren't going back to our room. My brother had just sent the elevator straight downstairs. This can't be right. I reach toward the panel to correct his mistake, but Christian grabs my wrist.

"Where are we going!?" I ask.

Christian glances at me, frowns, and then shrugs. "You'll see."

I open my mouth to complain as the elevator lurches to a stop. I waste no time throwing myself out between the prison-like metal doors. We cross the lobby and move into the parking lot. I emerge into the blinding sunlight and squint in the direction of my brother. He heads to the car, unlocks it, and pulls out a bag, the

"Emergency Bag." Just in case I start dying. It contains every kind of medical concoction that has ever been in my body or any reasonably small machine that has ever touched me. I back away from it immediately.

"Christian. Where are we going? Why do you need that?"

"Well, you know. Mom would kill me if you got hurt. And then we'd both be dead. So let's go!"

"Go where?" I yell. "I'm not supposed to go anywhere."

Christian scoffs. "You're not supposed to breathe without a doctor here to make sure you're doing it right."

"Did Mom and Dad approve of this?"

"To hell with what Mom and Dad approve of. I'm tired of this. You haven't seen the sun in years!" Christian retorts, jerking his chin toward my pale complexion.

"And?" I prompt.

My brother sighs. "We're going up the mountain."

"Up the—are you crazy?" I exclaim.

"We're not climbing the mountain. It's just a few minutes' hike through the forest. There's a nice path between the trees. It gets a little steep, but I know you can do it. There's something I want to show you. C'mon."

5

     I don't even fight Christian as he grabs my arm and hauls me off. Wait, let me correct myself: I can't fight him. He could pick me up if he needed to, I know that. I weigh about as much as a third grader. Besides, I'm still too shocked by his proposition to react.

     Before I know it, we're climbing up through the forest. The first part of the path is alright, I guess. A little cramped, but the wildlife and plants are beautiful. I relish the fresh air. Soon, the path starts to slope up. Christian underestimated my ability to climb anything more taxing than a moving escalator. I can barely breathe, and my vision starts to blur. I can nearly feel my muscles snapping with each step.

Death can't be as painful as this, my morbid thoughts complain. My heart, frantically trying to keep up with the physical activity and adrenaline, pumps anxiously in my chest. It has forgotten what real, moving blood feels like. Suddenly, a scorching flame rips through my lungs and I stop, bent over, hands on my knees. I'm nearly to the top of the hill, but I can't go any farther.

Christian, who has been following me, stops by my side. He's whistling. *Whistling.*

"What?" he asks, completely nonchalant.

I gasp. "I—I can't—"

"You can't what?" Christian sighs. *Why does he sound annoyed with me?* When your brother's dying, shouldn't you be more compassionate?

"Can't . . . go . . . any . . . farther . . ."

"Says who?"

"I'm not . . . supposed . . . to be . . . here."

"You'll be here if you want to be here!" Christian lashes out. He bends down and shoves his face into my vision. His features are so blurry I can barely separate him from the backdrop of trees. "No one can tell you what to do with your life," he continues harshly. "This whole time, there's been people dictating your actions. You know this, Andrew! You hate it! You hate it, and you still follow what they say! Why?"

I blink, clearing my vision. No one has ever spoken to me like this before. "They're trying to keep me alive," I grumble.

"I don't know about you, but what you have isn't much of a life," Christian retorts. Then, he straightens up and adds softly, "They're only protecting you until they strap you into the next hospital bed. What's the point? When you return there, will anything have changed? The world doesn't come around to see you, Andrew. It's the other way around."

I open my mouth to snap back at him, but nothing comes out. What can I say? Christian's right. What do I have to lose? Even if the worst does happen, isn't it better, anyway, to die out here than in a stark white hospital bed with beeping, indifferent machines? The forest doesn't feel like that. The forest is a representation of life.

Everything here is abundant with it, singing to me, urging me on.

Christian is standing behind me again. Ever so slowly, I straighten up and glance at his unflinching gaze. In that moment, I see something I've never seen before. Something that I didn't know I needed but had always been missing. Someone to believe in me. Someone who thought I could do it, even when I couldn't. I had only received pity before. Pity, or sadness, or my parents' worried faces. Christian's right. I am tired of it. There is still hope. My life might be able to have meaning after all.

6

I take a deep breath and start up the hill again. Christian gives a little cheer, but I can barely hear him. It is the hardest thing I have ever done. I don't have any feeling in more than half of my body. I can barely see where I'm going. The path is long and steep. The farther I climb, the rockier and more difficult it becomes. My breath has escaped me. I don't have a single second to chase it down. And I thought stairs were difficult.

Christian catches up with me and grabs my arm. I'm starting to trip more frequently. I close my eyes, and up we go. After a while, everything but the greenish-gold color of the forest shining through my eyelids disappears. I have to tune the pain out somehow, so I let my mind wander. It finds a peaceful, dark nook in the corner of my conscience and rests there.

Eventually, Christian tugs on my arm. I come to a jerking halt. Sweat is pouring down my back and face. I feel sticky and wet. My heartbeat pounds in my head, and my chest feels like it's on fire. My feet are barely strong enough to keep me up. My legs shake with exhaustion and victory. The pain is unbearable, thrilling, and strangely welcome. I stand there for a moment, relishing it. What a feeling, the feeling of being alive.

"So," I blearily hear Christian say over my shoulder, "what do you think?"

I look in the direction he's gesturing, and I can't believe my eyes. It is a beautiful sight. We are standing on a cliff. The forest recedes into green behind us, and in front of us, the jagged face of the mountain rises from a valley. A waterfall pounds down the side of the tall, craggy rock. Water splashes joyously into the river below. Flowers bloom everywhere. Green abounds. A bird flaps its wings loudly, and the sound echoes around us. The view takes away what little is left of my breath.

"It's . . . unbelievable," I pant. "How did you know it was here?"

"Mom and Dad. They had a brochure on the table. It mentioned this site for hikers. I thought they were going to let you see it, but as soon as they read about the path, I knew they wouldn't. So here you are. Hope you're not too disappointed."

"No it's . . . it's great," I gasp. Sensation slowly trickles back into my body. "Thank you."

I tip my face up into the golden, glittering light. So this was life. How different. And how close I had come to never having a taste of it. I throw my weary arms into the air and laugh aloud. As the waterfall splashes tiny droplets onto my face, I hear Christian join in, laughing behind me.

"You're welcome, Andrew."

I glance back at him and do my best impression of his grin. "Mom and Dad would kill us if they knew."

Christian grins back at me and shrugs. "Who cares what they think? You don't have to follow their every rule. You've never had to. They don't have the right to restrain experiences that aren't theirs. Let them know that you're capable of more than they think."

I smile. "Am I?"

Christian walks up behind me, rests his hand on my shoulder, and gives me a tight squeeze. "Of course you are. You just needed a little push out of the nest, don't you think?"

"That was spectacularly stupid," I grin at him. Then I pause a moment. I listen to the roaring water, regard the vitality of the forest, and savor the sensation of blood running through my veins. "But damn it feels good to fly."

About The Author

Linda Peng is a contributing author to the Storyshares library.

About The Publisher

Story Shares is a nonprofit focused on supporting the millions of teens and adults who struggle with reading by creating a new shelf in the library specifically for them. The ever-growing collection features content that is compelling and culturally relevant for teens and adults, yet still readable at a range of lower reading levels.

Story Shares generates content by engaging deeply with writers, bringing together a community to create this new kind of book. With more intriguing and approachable stories to choose from, the teens and adults who have fallen behind are improving their skills and beginning to discover the joy of reading. For more information, visit storyshares.org.

Easy to Read. Hard to Put Down.

A Set of Wings

www.ingramcontent.com/pod-product-compliance
Lightning Source LLC
Chambersburg PA
CBHW071230170626
46809CB00005BA/2002